CAT AND DOG
TAKE A TRIP

CAT AND DOG
TAKE A TRIP

CAT AND DOG TAKE A TRIP

BY ELIZABETH MILLER AND JANE COHEN
ILLUSTRATED BY VICTORIA CHESS

FRANKLIN WATTS/NEW YORK/LONDON/TORONTO/SYDNEY/1980

Library of Congress Cataloging in Publication Data

Miller, Elizabeth, 1933-
Cat and Dog take a trip.

SUMMARY: Despite the directions they've been given,
Cat, Dog, and Squirrel become lost on the way to visit
Rabbit in the city.
[1. Travel—Fiction.   2. English
language—Prepositions—Fiction.   3.
Vocabulary—Fiction.   4. Animals—Fiction]
I. Cohen, Jane, joint author.   II. Chess, Victoria.
III. Title.
PZ7.M6129Cay   [E]   80-14517
ISBN 0-531-03531-X
ISBN 0-531-04127-1 (lib. bdg.)

CAT AND DOG
TAKE A TRIP

Cat, Dog, and Squirrel were about to start an adventure.

They were going to the city to visit Rabbit. **Up** the
steps of the train went the three friends.

Dog bounded ahead and sat down **next to** the window. Cat plunked herself in the seat **next to** the aisle. Squirrel squeezed himself **in between** Cat and Dog.

As the train rolled toward the city, Cat said in her sweetest voice, "Dog, I think it's only fair that we take turns being **next to** the window." Dog got up immediately.

So did squirrel. But Cat got up faster and firmly settled herself **next to** the window.

Dog was now **next to** the aisle and poor squirrel
was left squashed in the **middle** again.

Squirrel, having nothing else to do, began to worry. "How are we going to find Rabbit's house when we get to the city?" asked Squirrel.

"Rabbit sent us directions. Let's look at them
again." Dog opened the suitcase.

On **top** were fresh cabbage leaves for Rabbit.

Dog dragged everything out to get the directions.

They were, of course, at the **bottom** of the suitcase.

Cat, muttering to herself, tried to jam all their things back **into** the suitcase.

The train arrived at the station.

Dog, Cat, and Squirrel climbed **down** the steps onto the platform.

"When you get off the train," Cat read, "you will be at the **bottom** of a hill. Go **up** the hill until you get to the **top**."

In **front** of them, just as Rabbit had said, was a
big hill. "There it is!" shouted Dog.

And he ran **up** to the **top** of the hill, where he had to stop and wait for Cat and Squirrel.

"From the **top** of the hill you will see a bridge.
Go **over** the bridge," read Cat.

From the **top** of the hill they could see the bridge, and off rushed Dog again, leaving Cat and Squirrel behind him.

"It would be faster to go **under** the bridge,"
thought Dog. So Dog went **under** the bridge.

Cat and Squirrel were shouting behind him,
"Over the bridge, Dog. We have to go **over** the bridge."

"We're lost," howled Dog.

Cat and Squirrel took Dog back **under** the bridge.

Then they went **over** the bridge, which was what Dog should have done in the first place.

"Turn right at the candy shop on the corner of Asparagus Avenue and Dandelion Lane. My house is number 8 Dandelion Lane. If I'm not home, the key will be on the shelf **over** the door." Cat tucked the directions in her purse. Dog nodded his head.

Sure enough, because they went **over** the bridge instead of **under** it, they soon came to the corner of Asparagus and Dandelion.

But Dog was off again, running. There it was — 8 Dandelion Lane. Dog had found the way!

Now all he had to do was get into the house. He rang the doorbell. No one answered. Dog began looking for the key.

He looked **under** the doormat.

Then he looked **in** the flower pot **on** the window ledge. There was no key anywhere!

Dog sat down **on** the steps in **front** of Rabbit's house. He had found the house but he could not get **in**.

Cat and Squirrel came puffing down the street.
"What's wrong, Dog?" Cat wheezed. "Why don't
you open the door?"

"I can't find the key," Dog moaned. "I looked **under** the doormat. I looked **in** the flower pot **on** the window ledge. The key is nowhere!"

"Did you look **over** the door where Rabbit said the key was?" asked Cat.

"Oh Cat, you're right. Now I remember. Rabbit said the key was **over** the door."

Dog reached **up, over** the door. There it was!
The beautiful brass key.

Rabbit came home soon and brought many friends with him. They had a delicious carrot salad for dinner with fresh cabbage leaves on **top**. Dog, Cat, Squirrel, and Rabbit and his friends had a fine feast.

**Fun learning adventures
with Cat and Dog:**

CAT AND DOG GIVE A PARTY
(learn to count)

CAT AND DOG HAVE A CONTEST
(learn primary colors)

CAT AND DOG AND THE MIXED-UP WEEK
(learn the days of the week)

CAT AND DOG RAISE THE ROOF
(learn shapes)

CAT AND DOG TAKE A TRIP
(learn basic directions)